Strawberry Kisses

A 1Night Stand Story

By
Dominique Eastwick

Dedication

This book is dedicated to Valerie Mann who never ever let me give up on my writing and who pushed me to give my best. Thanks, Val

And of course, to my own personal Hero, my husband.

Chapter One

Mia blew out a frustrated sigh and stared at the mess around her feet. Flyers and promotional posters littered the carpet in a three hundred and sixty degree radius. Crouching down, she assessed the chaos with frustrated bemusement.

"Could you be a dear and take some of this with you, Mia?" she mimicked in the deep voice of Kendal Huxton, owner and slave driver for Baron Gaming, Inc. "Idiot."

"Excuse me?"

Mia glanced up from the squatting position, blew the stray hair out of her eyes while being mesmerized by what had to be the sexiest blue eyes pair she had ever seen. This was the kind of man she programmed into the games she created. This was the hero, the one everyone played to get the gold, kill the dragon, and if they were lucky, win the loot.

"Sorry, not you—I meant me. I'm the idiot."

His deep laugh reverberated through her all the way down to her flip-flopped, purple-painted toes. "Here, let me help you with these."

She nodded, not able to say much past the lump in her throat anyway. She watched the dark wool fabric of his pants pull tight over his thighs, and try as she might not to, her gaze followed the inseam of his pants to rest on his crotch. Her overactive imagination went into overdrive wondering what this man would look like minus his clothes. With her cheeks burning, she turned away knowing her face had to be the same color as the rose carpet under her feet. Swiping her hands over the pamphlets, she pulled them into a bigger pile before her.

"Here." He handed her the glossy 8 x 10 posters for *Fantasy Realms: Age of the Dragons*. "With so many copies of these, you're either a huge stalker-like fan of this game, or you're one of the girls hired to turn on young boys at the gamers' convention."

She didn't know how to take the comment—nothing about her screamed sex kitten hired to turn on anyone, and it had been a long time since she'd been thought of as a girl. Before she could answer, a beautiful woman—weren't *they all here in Vegas?*—*grabbed* the sex god by the arm and tugged.

"You'll be late if we don't leave soon."

He glanced at his watch and shrugged "She's right. She usually is. I am going to be late for my date." He pointed at the papers on the floor. "You got this?"

Disappointment engulfed Mia. "Yes, thank you for helping."

"And thank you for not calling *me* an idiot. Can I take one of these? My son is a huge fan of the game. He says their designer, Miriam Callrous, is his hero and he wants to design games just like she does when he grows up."

Fumbling through the pile, she grabbed a few posters and reached out to give them to him. "Sure, take as many as you like."

"One should do it. He probably got one signed today, anyway. He has been at the convention all afternoon with one of his buddies."

"Oh no, the autograph signing is tomorrow, if you want...."

"G , we've got to go." The woman grew more insistent and annoying by the minute. Good lord, didn't she know Mia wanted him for just one second more? *That's it, one second—is that too much to ask?*

"Take a Valium, Sylvia." "G" threw a frustrated look at the beautiful woman before standing up, causing Mia to strain her neck to see his face. He tapped the poster in his hand once. "Thanks again."

Yes, it was too much to ask. She sat on the floor of the very expensive hotel, watching the man of her fantasies walk away with a beautiful woman, on his way to give something to his son before going on a date. Wow, even for her that seemed fucked up. And exactly why she preferred her small house in the middle of nowhere with her two dogs, three cats, half dozen chickens and her state of the art, every-gadget-you-could-think-of computer system.

She gathered up the remaining papers in a disorganized heap, hit the elevator up button with her elbow, and smiled a smile she didn't feel when the elevator attendant asked her what floor. And while she watched the numbers move toward the thirty-fifth floor, she exhaled a second sigh of frustration.

Mia understood ROM, RAM, hard drives, html codes and anything that had to do with computers. Hell she could create larger-than-life animated characters for her games that people loved and wanted to become, or as the army of gamers refer to them as simply "toons", But with all her knowledge of what made real men and women want her toons, she didn't relate those same *real* people well at all. And that was why she had, at the urging of her ever nosy, always loving, and very pregnant-for-the-seventh-time sister, agreed to sign up for the dating site, 1NightStand.

1NightStand, the exclusive, high-end dating service for people with money who couldn't find a date on their own. The reviews for Madame Eve's services were spectacular and guaranteed an experience both discreet and without embarrassment. So tonight, she had a date, and though that didn't mean sex was in the cards, her odds were stacked higher for it tonight than they had been in years. And she was in Vegas, so if she couldn't take a gamble there, where else could she?

Her happily married sister thought her single sister needed to get laid by something that didn't require batteries. And to be honest, it had been a very long time since a real man had touched her, let alone brought her any kind of pleasure. Hell, it had been a long time since a man showed any interest in her at all. She might be a teenage gaming boy's wet dream, but she seemed to leave most grown men limp.

She exited the elevator and headed down the long hall to her suite, a suite that with any luck she wouldn't be sleeping in tonight.

Chapter Two

Gavin threw his cell phone on the king-size bed. She was late, over thirty minutes late, and he had a sneaking suspicion he'd been stood up. Which was actually fine with him since the woman from the convention center earlier kept popping into his head. With her full lips and fuller curves, she'd made him hard within a second of talking to her. He'd asked for the poster not because he knew his son would love it, but to hide the raging erection he showed the world.

She was everything he loved in a woman, soft and round where she should be soft and round. His tastes in the ladies always ran with larger, more feminine ones, rather than skinny, boyish girls. And perhaps that was the major reason things hadn't worked out with his waiflike ex-wife Janice. He wanted someone he wasn't afraid to fuck hard for fear of breaking. When Janice had been pregnant with their son, he'd been in heaven, but she'd been miserable, and the few times she'd allowed him access to her body, she'd complained the whole time. Nothing was a bigger turn off than a woman who pointed out all her flaws. Flaws he as a man found appealing.

But this woman seemed comfortable in her skin—she didn't wear a lot of make up and though she hadn't been showing much skin, what little he had seen sent his blood pressure skyrocketing. If his suspicions that the night's date wasn't going to work out came true, he would simply track down his mysterious gamer girl. Since he knew which company she was there with as well as where she would be, he had every plan to track her down the next day.

When thirty minutes came and went, he texted Madame Eve, the mysterious owner of the exclusive dating service 1Night Stand to tell her he was out of there. He took one more look around the room, picked up his worn black leather overnight bag, and headed down the hallway to the door. The familiar chime of his phone told him he had a text waiting. Instead of a message begging him to understand, or saying she would set him up with someone else, he found one requesting he stay and give it some time.

Be patient, mon chère, sometimes what we most want doesn't always get there when we expect it to. You must trust me, if you wait just a little while longer you will not regret it. I promise you that.

"Fine," he said to the air, throwing the bag onto the dresser top and pacing the room. God help him from meddlesome sisters. Sylvia insisted he check out the dating site, which he had. She was convinced he'd lost his mind and been quite vocal about it when he mentioned he could just ask the poster woman from the convention out instead of coming on this date.

So there he stood, in a beautifully decorated room of the world-class family Castillo Resort, waiting to pay to get laid by one woman while lusting for another. Quite a feat for a man who hadn't been interested in anything sexual in almost five years. When his wife left him for her co-worker three years earlier, their relationship had been dead for years already. The only shock for him that she'd actually been having sex at all, much less with someone else.

What sounded like a cement brick crashed outside the door, grabbing his attention and pulling him out of his musings. Without a thought, he threw open the door to find *her*, the woman from his thoughts, sitting on the floor, throwing an assortment of things into a large, ugly, very utilitarian bag. He blinked twice and shook his head, trying to shake the suspicion he might be hallucinating.

"Idiot."

Nope, no hallucination, definitely her. "I think we've been through this before, unless of course you actually are calling me an idiot this time."

"You?" Her head shot up, and her mouth dropped open for a quick second before she composed herself and started shoveling items back into her bag with little success.

"Me."

"What are you doing here?" Her beautiful green eyes locked with his and his cock came to life again.

"I suspect the same thing you are."

"But you have a date." She appeared so

perplexed he wanted to kiss her senseless.

"Yes, and I believe it's with you." *I couldn't be so lucky.* "You must be Mia?"

"That's me."

"Mia, I'm Gavin." He held out his hand, and when she placed her soft, smaller one in his, he gave a gentle tug to urge her to her feet. Moving her hand to his lips, he turned it over and placed a gentle kiss over the inside of her wrist. Her heat warmed his lips and she inhaled sharply. He smiled. "Come on in."

Bending down, he grabbed her bag, threw what remained on the floor unceremoniously back into it, waited just outside the doorway until she walked into the room, then shut it behind them. She touched the wallpaper, her fingers grazing the silk, much like he hoped they'd graze his hard cock. She walked around the room, taking it all in, but it wasn't lost on him that her eyes avoided the huge bed. With its overstuffed pillows and thick comforter, plus the gigantic headboard, he wondered how she thought he wouldn't notice her apprehension.

Not that it mattered, because he was quite content to fuck her against the wall, in the chair, or even on the floor at that point. His hormones and certain parts of his body had decided they'd waited long enough for him to come to his senses. They were taking over.

He watched like a starving man as she moved further into the room, her full hips swaying back and forth as she walked over to the sheer cream silk curtains that let the fading light from the Nevada sun glow over her. He waited. There was something in her body language, tight with nerves, that he couldn't read. He wasn't sure if she was anxious for the evening or ready to bolt. It would kill him to let her walk away, so he needed to play it cool, take it slowly.

"So how does this work?" She asked, her fingertips caressing the fabric.

"How does what work?" Had she noticed the hitch in his voice? He debated whether to hide his erection or let her see what effect she had on him.

"So, do we get naked and go at it like teenagers left alone in an empty house, or do we chat and get to know each other first?"

Feeling like a randy schoolboy, talking didn't really sound like much of a plan, but he wasn't sure telling her that would be wise. "I don't think there are any set rules we have to follow. If you want to chat, we can do that. Personally, I would like to get to know you in other ways as well."

"So it would seem." She nodded toward his crotch, one brown eyebrow raised and a smirk forming on her full lips.

A knock on the door saved him from answering. In fact, he wasn't sure he could have answered her anyway. His mouth became dry and his core temperature rose. Turning away, he wondered what made him worry she'd run, and he could only be thankful for his good blessings that she seemed as eager as he was for what the night had in store for them.

***

Mia watched him walk to the door. He had an ass to die for, her hands itching to squeeze the two perfect buns. Getting hold of herself, she turned back to the window and watched the Vegas Strip come to life in the final fading light of day, mentally tallying the endless hotels with endless rooms. Behind her, she heard the door close with a click and knew they were alone again.

"Did you know there are one hundred forty eight thousand, nine hundred and forty one hotel rooms in Las Vegas?" she said, as matter of fact as if it was a normal conversation to be had in a high class room, with a man who'd paid for a "date" with her. One she had also paid a pretty penny for. That he was paying to get to know her stunned her, since he was a man she would have thought had no trouble getting a date in the conventional way. The fact he was there baffled as much as it intrigued.

"I did not know that." His voice was closer then she expected and she turned to find him directly in front of her. "Madame Eve sent us a gift."

Mia glanced at the rolling table and the bottle of chilled champagne. He lifted the silver-domed cover to reveal a plate of the juiciest, largest strawberries she had ever seen, surrounding a bowl of melted chocolate. She was afraid for a moment she might have groaned out loud. "How do you know it's from her?"

"She left us a note." He handed it to her.

Remember, be patient mon chères, enjoy your time together. You have all evening.

Mia glanced at him, about to ask if he knew what the note meant, but the glimmer in his eyes told her he wasn't going to say any more. Instead, he dipped one of the ruby red strawberries into the dark chocolate. His gaze darted to her mouth as she licked her bottom lip.

"Here." His voice took on a deeper, husky tone as he brought the berry to her mouth, the warm chocolate invading her senses. She sucked the tip of the strawberry for a minute before letting her teeth take over, the rush of sweet juice and the smooth taste, sweet and thick, slipping over her tongue.

Giggling, she started to wipe the liquid away, but he was quicker, using his mouth and tongue to suck the juice off gently.

Deep down in her belly, butterflies stirred, hundreds, if not thousands. At that moment, she wasn't sure if she should make the next move or if he would. He'd made it clear he desired her. She wanted him, had since she'd first laid eyes upon him. Just as she made her decision to move in for a full kiss, he pulled away and grabbed the bottle.

Disappointment racked her as she took her own step back. What did that say about her if after one kiss, he was reaching for the alcohol.

"Do you want the next strawberry with chocolate, or champagne?" He popped the cork.

"I, um...." She slowed her breathing, trying hard to concentrate on his words. "I've never had champagne and strawberries."

"Really?" As he smiled, the first real smile she'd seen on his face was breathtaking, She could only nod since somewhere between her mouth and her brain she'd lost the ability to form simple words.

Pouring one glass of the bubbly wine, he took a sip, smiled then grabbed another plump berry. He rubbed it slightly on her lower lip. "Take a bite."

He didn't have to tell her twice. She bit, then savored, as he raised the flute and tilted it just enough for her to get a swallow of the liquid. Her eyes widened as the tastes of the fruit and champagne fused in her mouth.

"Another bite then?" He didn't wait for her

answer, giving her another piece and let her enjoy the fruit for what it was, savoring and treasuring as some of the best she'd ever had.

She opened her eyes just in time to see his close, and his mouth settle over hers. Her lips parted and a rush of champagne from his mouth filled her own. The fizzy liquid overwhelmed her senses. If she could have let out an *ooh*, she would have. But all she could think about was his tongue dancing with hers. His left hand still holding the flute, he wrapped it around her waist, pulling her closer. She felt the heat of his erection at the same time his rigid cock pressed against her belly.

Pulling away enough to wind her arms around his neck, she prevented any escape on his part. She had him where she wanted him no matter how good the strawberries or the champagne, wanted him right there, kissing her. He didn't fight her, instead deepening the kiss. She breathed in, his scent acting like an aphrodisiac on her already hyper libido, bringing her to the brink of ripping his clothes off and jumping his cock right then.

His arm left her waist for a minute—she heard

the clink of the flute on the table, but his lips never left hers. She melted into him as his warm palms cupped her heated cheeks, forcing her mind back to the kiss.

"Tell me what you want?" His breath was warm against her lips.

"I want you."

"How? Give me permission, tell me it's okay to strip you naked, kiss you wherever the need takes me, and fuck you until you can't see straight."

"Yes, yes, please, all of that."

It was all the encouragement he needed. His warm hands palmed her breasts, weighing them, his thumbs working the nipples to hard nubs under the layers of clothing she wore. Letting her head fall back, she savored the feel of his hands on her, of a man's hands, warm and strong on her long-starved body.

The exposed line of her neck seemed to be too much temptation for him to turn away from. His hot mouth descended on the shallow spot at the base of her throat, one hand pulling her into even more intimate contact with his body, while the other never stopped working its magic on her breast. But his mouth—he had a mouth that could make a woman forget her own name.

"You can touch me, too. In fact, really, I wish you would," he growled.

Flushed with desire, she moved her hands from his shoulders and down his hard chest to an equally solid stomach. He amazed her. He'd said he had an older son, so that meant he was in his late thirties at the very least, but the speckles of gray mixed within his dark brown hair told her he was probably closer to forty, and yet he had the body of a twenty year old. She couldn't help being happy, however, that his experience was of the thirty or forty year old. She wanted a man who knew what to do with what he had.

His eyes darkened, glued to hers as she explored his torso with fingers eager to learn every curve and plane, With his gaze giving her the courage to do what she fantasized about, she pulled his shirt from the confines of his pants and let her fingers touch his heated skin. His hissed as they made the first contact. Her unsteady hands undid one button at a time, bringing her lips down over the exposed skin as the shirt opened and allowed her more access to his well-sculpted chest. Finishing the task at hand, she pushed the shirt off his shoulders. He released the cufflinks at his wrists with quick finesse, pulling the shirt the rest of the way off and tossing it on the nearest chair.

Mia couldn't take her eyes off the man before her, his muscular body exactly what she designed her warrior men in her video games to be. Both her hands skimmed down over his hard, well-defined pecs to his rippled abs. Her left hand played with the edge of the waistband of his pants as her right hand moved down over his hips and then to the center, cupping and feeling the large erection threatening to break the zipper. He was perfect.

It was her last thought before the world spun and his mouth found hers again. She landed on her back on the large bed she'd done her best to avoid noticing as she came in. His hands moved up her legs, pushing the skirt as he went, his mouth never leaving hers. When he met with bare skin past her thigh-high nylons, he groaned deep. Pulling away, he flipped her to the side, undid the fastenings on her skirt, and shimmied it over her hips and down her legs.

The cool air hit her skin, sent a shiver up her spine, and caused goose pimples to cover her body, not sexy, definitely not the response she hoped for. But he didn't seem to care, his eyes focused on her spread legs, clad only in black silk thigh highs, and her pussy covered by the thinnest of fabrics. She moved to lift her sweater over her head, but he delayed her.

"No, not yet. I wish I could describe how incredibly sexy you are, my fantasy come to life. On the outside you're conservative and reserved, but underneath you're fire and brimstone and sex on heels."

His fingers moved over the silk fabric covering her most intimate of places, running under the edge much like her fingers had run along his waistband. The look of shock over his face made her glad she had followed her sister's advice.

"Holy hell," he muttered, pulling down the thong underwear and gazing upon her shaved lips, full and wanting with sexual need.

He pushed her knees wider, his eyes never

leaving the apex between her thighs. In the past it may have made her self-conscious, but his bold, sexy stare made her feel like every man's fantasy. He kneeled on the edge of the bed, hooking her knees over his shoulders, and grabbed her hips, pulling her toward the edge of the bed. His fingers moved into the folds of her pussy lips, coming in contact with the evidence of her passion, wet and eager for him.

One finger entered her, moving at an achingly slow pace, and she clenched her walls around his finger, needing more, wanting so much, and so very hot she wasn't sure that one finger wouldn't put her over the edge. Her hips moved up of their own accord.

"What do you want, Mia?"

"More," she gasped, unable to say another word.

"Of this?" He placed a second finger beside the first. "Perhaps you want this as much as I do."

Before the words could sink in, his mouth was on her swollen clit, sucking, his tongue doing things she couldn't have imagined. She gripped the bed linens with such force her fingertips grew numb. She didn't want to come so quickly, but as she felt the first flutters of her release deep in her belly, she panted, every breath an effort to slow down the impending explosion building deep within her womb. Every nerve in her body came to beautiful, electric life.

He placed his free hand on her stomach, his warm palm radiating heat deep into her, then added pressure to her womb. She exploded, throwing her head back but unable to make a sound. Had she been able to, she was certain she'd have shattered ,and not even the healing buffs from the most epic of healers in her game would have been able to put the pieces back together when she did.

Only his hand, firm and strong on her body, kept her from flying off the bed. And just as she floated down, right when she could breathe again, he added a third and then a fourth finger, and his thumb and tongue worked her up to another peak.

This time she did scream, afraid the person in the next room would call security. She cried his name and said words she'd never said in the company of a man before. The orgasm rode over her, through her. Over and over, the electric flood took her until she thought she'd drown.

When the shaking subsided and her world came back into focus, she found Gavin staring at her in awe and masculine pleasure. She covered her face with her arm as embarrassment heated her face.

"You are so amazingly beautiful when you come. I have never seen anything like that."

Pulling up on her elbows, she searched his eyes, waiting for something—some sign that he was teasing, playing with her, leading her on. Yet the only thing hiding in his deep blue eyes was honesty and adoration. *Why was it that this man who I only have one night with can make me feel what no other man has managed in all my years?* He made her feel sexy and alluring.

Willing her body to move, since all the energy had been sucked out of her with the last orgasm, she pushed herself to the edge of the bed. Sitting with one leg on either side of him, Mia met his gaze. His breathing was unsteady, as if fighting to get air to his lungs—he seemed as out of breath as she was. And if she had anything to say about it, he'd be out of breath even more in the next few minutes.

Her fingers worked at his belt, slowly and

painstakingly removing it from his belt loops. Then, gently, she undid the button and zipper, letting the expensive wool pants puddle at his feet. She moved off the bed and lifted each foot, removed his socks then pushed the pants out of the way. She let her hand sculpt and knead the muscles of his legs as she worked her way up to his waist and sat back on the edge of the bed. His raging hard-on begged for relief.

"You don't have to...."

"I want to," Mia said with a smile, and found to her shock and amazement it was the complete truth—for the first time in her adult life the thought of taking a cock deep into her mouth didn't turn her off, but had an erotic, even naughty appeal. Truth be told, she'd never enjoyed giving head. Sure, she read the romance novels where the heroine lost herself in the process, but Mia always wanted it over and done with. In the past, the thought of having a man come in her mouth or on her tits had never been a turn on. But she was a big believer in quid pro quo, and he'd just given her the two most amazing orgasms of her life. The least she could do was return the favor.

Taking a centering breath, she playfully let her

fingers move around the waistband of his black briefs. His muscles tightened under her touch and she couldn't help running her hand down his muscular bottom. His ass remained tight for a second before relaxing again. She teased him and he allowed it, never once demanding, although his eyes pleaded a little and he appeared unsure where to place his fisted hands. Everything about his response gave her a power surge and upped her feminine prowess.

Hooking the briefs, she inched them down past his hips until finally she moved over his cock. It might not have been the largest she had seen, but it was thick and, in fact the most beautiful cock she had ever laid eyes on. Without further thought, she lowered her mouth to the tip and let her tongue taste him. Instead of being repulsed, she was intrigued. Instead of the bitter taste she had expected, it was slightly salty with a sweet tinge.

Closing her eyes, she took his thick cock between her lips and let her tongue lick over the head, lapping up the beads of pre-cum. The more that came, the more she wanted. She put her hands on his ass cheeks because she wanted to touch them again and it also allowed her some control over how deep she took him into her mouth, moving up and down until the head touched the back of her throat and he groaned. His hands, once tight at his sides, fisted in her hair, teaching her what he liked.

"I won't last much longer."

Don't care. She would never have believed she'd enjoy giving a man oral sex, but the blowjob turned her on all over again. Her juices pooled between her legs and her nipples hardened to painful buds.

He tried to pull away. He was close to the edge, his legs shaking with the need to release, his gorgeous ass clinched tight, like a rock in her palms. She continued lapping his cock, never giving up, never giving him an inch. His cock twitched as she brought her lips to the head and she looked up to see his eyes closed, his jaw tight. She wanted him to lose all control the way she had. She needed him to feel the ecstasy that she'd felt. Reluctant to leave his ass, it really was an amazing ass after all, she moved one hand around front to cup his balls.

He let out his breath in a loud hiss between clenched teeth and started to pump into her mouth with fervor. His breathing became erratic, his fingers tightening in her hair. He was so close. As his need to come increased, her need to bring him there doubled.

This time she wanted it, this time she needed to taste him. She pulled his hips forward, taking him as deep as she could, and the first spurt of cum hit the back of her throat. With his cock deep, she glanced up at him. His eyes were closed and his jaw tight, he made not a sound and didn't seem to even be breathing. If not for his pulsating penis she would have thought he had been hit by a freeze spell from one of her games. She swallowed until he finally moved, placing his hands on her shoulders and nearly collapsing with the relief of his orgasm.

She let him go then and licked her lips to get whatever had escaped. His face showed his awe, and with shaky movements he took a few steps toward the bed, falling on it. With a satisfied groan, he hooked an arm around her to bring her with him. "We have all night and I think I'm done in already.'

"Oh, no you don't. We still have twelve hours, and I want everything I can get from you."

Gavin's laughter vibrated against her chest and

to her core. *It's just sex, just amazing, crazy sex.* But closing her eyes, she knew it was more, and if she let him take a piece of her heart, he would take it all, and in the morning she would be left alone—again.

His lips grazed her forehead while his fingers traced over and under her exposed breast. She moaned, the familiar tingle between her thighs coming to roaring life again. Her moan was met by his groan as he rolled over her. Soft lips took hers in a hungry, possessive lip-lock that left her breathless and eager for more. His tongue invaded her mouth and left her no choice but to concede to his demands. One muscular leg eased hers apart until he settled between her thighs, his erection hard and hot against her apex.

"You make me feel like a teenager again," he said against her neck as his lips left burning kisses in their wake. His trail led to her breasts, her nipples hard and wanting, aching for his attention , every molecule of her body alive under his attentions. She curled her hips up to meet his.

He pulled away from her and his eyes took in her ample curves. His lips took hers again for a quick kiss before he pushed away and left the bed, leaving her fumbling and confused. "Where...."

"Condoms." He snatched a box out of his bag then headed for the table by the window.

"And now?"

"Strawberries." He grabbed the bowl from the table and came back to her, placing the condoms within reach, but holding on to the strawberries. Taking one plump fruit in his fingers, he held it to her lips, encouraging her to take a nibble. She bit the tip, savoring the taste, feeling the juice dribble over her lips until her tongue caught the liquid.

He moved the strawberry over her right nipple, circling it until the hard nub was wet and sticky with the sweet, red juice. It ran down the side of her breast, only stopping when he caught it with his soft tongue, licking his way back to the peaked nipple. He repeated the action on the other breast, sending shivers down her spine, leaving goose pimples over her heated flesh. Savoring the feel of his tongue and mouth on her body, she found it hard to keep her head up. Yet there was something erotic about studying him feast on her, compelling her to stay focused on him, even when all she wanted was to throw back her head and feel.

Taking the remaining berry into his mouth, he moved back up her body until his lips met hers again. He kissed her, letting her savor his unique taste mixed with that of the berry. She would never eat a strawberry again without thinking about him, about that moment and knew every time she walked by a strawberry stand she'd get wet. Something so innocent would forever hold an importance to that one, unforgettable night.

"Please, I want you," she begged, wrapping her legs around his hips. Her heels urged him down and forward.

"Patience, Mia. We have all night."

"I haven't felt patient around you since the moment you helped me pick up those brochures, and that was hours ago. I've been patient enough." She lifted her hips, letting her pussy rub against his hard cock.

With a groan he pulled away, leaving her for a moment to grab the foil package. He opened it with his white teeth, smiling at her. Lifting her up on her elbows, she watched in rapture as he sheathed his cock, rolling the condom down its length with slow precision. His hand stroked up one more time before he came down on her with a feral growl.

His hand wrapped around the back of her thigh, pulling her leg up and out giving him more access to her wet, wanting pussy. Again she shifted her hips, but instead of pulling back he surged forward, taking her breath away. She felt full and complete for the first time in years.

Their eyes met, locked, and she couldn't tear hers away from the depths of his blue ones. He drank her in as he pushed into her again. His breath came out on a rush of hot air as she clenched around his rigid cock. He pulled away from her so he could watch himself enter her body. Lifting his hips, he inched out of her to the tip, making her crazy with want and desire before entering her again. He repeated the action, once, twice, three times before coming down full body on her, his mouth taking hers with the desire and need his cock inflamed. He took complete possession of her then took her to heights she'd never experienced. Before she could fall over the edge into oblivion, he reined her in, pulling the glorious sexual torture out.

She begged him for more and in equal measure pleaded with him to stop. She didn't want to the sensation to end, but wasn't sure how much she could take and still be whole. Everything about the evening felt like fate had stepped in. And maybe it had. *Maybe, just maybe, fate wants me to have mind-blowing, eye-crossing, unbelievable sex, and who am I to argue?*

Gavin stroked faster, his breathing more labored. She was so close, and so was he. The vixen she never imagined living inside her wrapped her legs around his waist, her heels resting on his buttocks, pushing, forcing him deeper.

"Oh hell, Gavin, fuck me. Harder, please."

"Oh shit." His eyes closed, his brow furrowed. His hand moved over her curved thigh to find her full ass—he grabbed it, changing the angle of his entrance ever so slightly, pushing the base of his cock against her swollen clit. She flew high and over the edge, a starburst starting in her abdomen and shooting through her veins. Over and over the waves crashed, surrounded her, took control until they left her limp and exhausted. So caught up in her ecstasy after her free fall, she hadn't realized Gavin had gone over with her. He lay on top of her, his head on her shoulder, his breath hot against her neck.

Her nails gently scored his back from buttocks to shoulder and down again, reveling in the tiny goose pimples left in their wake. He tried to move off of her, pushed up on his arms, allowing her to see his face and savor his handsome features, but she didn't want him to leave, didn't want to loose the contact. She was exhausted and he had to be too, but she was afraid this was the one and only time they would share this together and suddenly that wasn't enough for her. She wanted more.

So she held on, let him fall back against her, and he stayed where he was. When she heard the gentle soft snore against her ear, she smiled, her own heavy lids falling and joining into a deep, sated sleep, her last thought—he smelled like strawberries.

Chapter Three

G avin woke refreshed—he hadn't felt so good in years. Reaching beside him, he hoped to wake Mia for another round of mind-blowing sex, but instead found a cold, empty bed. Sitting up, he listened for the telltale sound of water running in the bathroom, but heard nothing. In fact, the room was eerily quiet.

Throwing his feet over the edge, he glanced for a minute at the closed bathroom door, in his heart knew no one was in there, but a kernel of hope still clung that maybe, just maybe she would be. He took his time moving the five paces it took to get from the bed to the bathroom, glaring at the offending door, knowing he looked like a complete idiot staring at the it as though it were about to fight back. Pushing it open, he found the room dark, and as he expected, empty. Cursing under his breath, he walked to the window and threw back the curtains to stare at the Strip below. What had she said? Something like one hundred thousand rooms in Las Vegas and how the hell was he supposed to find her in one of them? It would take him at least an hour to get into the convention then getting through the crowd to the booth she worked would take even longer. If his son knew all about that company, then so did every geek, gamer and techie there.

Why the hell hadn't she just woken him up? He would have told her he wanted more than one night. They could have exchanged numbers. Something—hell, *anything*.

Running his hands through his hair in disgust, he turned from the window to assess the once-immaculate room. The empty champagne bottle and the remnants of the strawberries still sat on the table. His clothes lay haphazard around the room, evidence that he hadn't cared where they landed as long as they weren't on his body. He picked up his shirt, then his tie, following the trail that led straight to the bed.

Defeated and frustrated, he sat on the edge. Angry at himself for letting one night with a woman he knew only in the biblical sense get so far under his skin. Angry at her for not having the common courtesy or courage to look him in the face when she walked away.

Then his eyes caught something. Stuck between the mirror and its frame was an envelope. Scribbled on the paper was his name, nearly illegible in the chicken scratch. His lips twitched until he laughed out loud with joy. He hadn't even read the letter, but he basked in the knowledge she hadn't slunk out of the room, but had taken the time to pen a note. That had to be something.

Moving far faster across the room than he had only moments before, he reached for the envelope and ripped it open. Pulling out a piece of hotel stationary, his eyes adjusted to the messy script before attempting to read it all.

Tried to wake you...okay, I didn't try hard. I really overslept and was afraid if I woke you, I would miss work. As much as I don't want to go, I contractually have to. Included are three tickets to the expo and VIP passes for you, your son, and his friend to get into the Fantasy Realms chat. If you are interested in more, please come. If not....

Thanks for a wonderful night,

Mia

Glancing at the bedside clock, he headed for the bathroom, but not before grabbing his cell and calling his son to tell him that he had a huge surprise waiting for him, and to meet him outside the convention center in an hour.

***

Mia wrung her hands together—after all these years and the number of times she had spoken on panels, she should be used to it. But she never was. Fans could get brutal when expansions came out, and they were vocal. They knew the ins and outs of the story and if she missed something, she'd be fried for it. Added to that stress was whether or not Gavin would show. She'd taken the coward's way out that morning, and she admitted it.

When she'd woken and seen the time, she'd

nearly had a heart attack. She shook him once to say she had to leave, but when his arm came around her, urging her into a kiss, she knew she'd never get out. It was for the best. She didn't have to look him in the eye and say *thanks for a great night and a great lay*, as he admitted that was all he wanted from her.

But now she wondered if she'd be able to concentrate on the questions, remember what the story line was, and keep from shaking as her nerves took over.

She entered the room to the sound of applause and waved. The flash cameras blinded her and she tripped up the stairs. Thankfully, one of the actors dressed as a warrior from the game grabbed her arm and helped her up the few remaining steps. Smiling, she sat in the chair that had her name before it on the table. Seated to the side of her were two of the other head designers, the director, and the famous actors who voiced the main characters.

As the lights faded to allow better viewing of the premier of the trailer for *Fantasy Realms: Age of the Dragons*, Mia reached for her water glass, hoping to ease some of her nervousness. The actor to her left, whose name she couldn't remember, leaned in and complimented her on the graphics. She managed to smile and nod and croak out a thank you before it dawned on her that in the dark he couldn't see her nod.

After two minutes of cinematic graphic overload, the lights came back up and the room was silent. Her heart sank. Then she saw him—Gavin. He stood and clapped, followed by the rest of the room erupting in loud woots and cheers. He smiled at her then bowed his head before sitting down again.

For the next forty-five minutes, nothing seemed to matter, her whole focus on Gavin sitting in the back of the room. She answered questions and hoped what she said made sense. Only when the people in front of Gavin got up did it dawn on her that the session had come to an end.

She moved around the actors and toward the steps of the stage. Eager to get to the other end of the room to talk with Gavin, her eyes stayed on the door to assess if he'd left, but through the throng of people she couldn't tell. When she finally made it through the group, many eager to talk with her, she was disappointed to find Gavin's row vacant. He'd left and she had no idea how to contact him otherwise. She didn't know his last name, didn't know what hotel he was at.

Defeated, she sat down in the chair he had been sitting in. "Idiot."

"Again with the idiot?" His rough voice sent a thrill to her toes.

"Gavin." She jumped up and turned to her left.

One eyebrow raised and his lips curved up into a cheeky smile. "Mia, or should I call you *Miriam*?"

"No, Mia, always Mia."

"Well, Always Mia."

"Dad!" The teenage boy beside Gavin groaned. "Don't be a noob."

"Noob?" Gavin asked his son.

Mia found it hard not to laugh—the look of complete confusion was so endearing and comical at the same time. "It's a gamer's term. Means basically *don't be lame.*"

"Ah. Mia, this is my son, Grady, and his friend Alan."

She hated taking her eyes off Gavin, but with a

big smile she glanced at the thinner, younger version of him. "It's a pleasure to meet you both."

"Oh, my God, you have no idea how cool this is. No one will believe I met you." Grady pulled his phone out of his pocket and pointed it at Mia, clicking a quick picture.

"Oh, I doubt anyone would be that interested. But...." She smiled before moving to stand beside the boys. She grabbed Grady's cell phone, leaned in near him, and took a picture. "Now they have proof. Meet me at the booth in an hour and I'll get you hooked up with all sorts of gear."

"Epic! Dad, can we go back to the convention floor?"

"Yeah, I'll meet up with you at Mia's booth."

The boys didn't wait to get out the door before they were texting on their phones. Tension filled Mia as the buffer of the kids was gone, very aware she and Gavin were the only two left in the room.

"You've made their day."

"I can't imagine why." When her eyes met his, she forgot what else she planned to say. All she wanted was to feel his soft lips on hers again.

"You have no idea how angry I was when I woke up alone."

"Sorry, I...."

"Was a chicken?"

"Yes, though scaredy-cat might be closer to the truth."

Gavin took a step closer to her and she inhaled, smelling his unique scent, mixed with his expensive cologne. "What were you scared of?"

"I didn't know. I still don't know if you want more. Or if one night was enough." She hated feeling unsure of herself. She hated not knowing what was in his mind, Yes, he had come to her, but maybe only because of his son. Maybe Gavin, unlike her, was the type of person to say things face-to-face.

"What if I said I wanted more then just last night? That I wanted to give us a chance, to see where this might go?"

"I would say okay." Unable to look at him for fear he would see every last emotion laid bare in her eyes, she lowered her face to focus on the cheap ring on her pinkie.

"Just okay?" His voice was soft and she closed

her eyes as he placed his finger below her chin and forced her to look at him. When she opened her lids, reflected in his blue pools were the same emotions she felt.

A blush rose over her cheeks. "I would say yes, please. Then I would say, I want more, so much more, I nearly blew off today to spend the day in bed with you."

"I wish you had."

"Will you please kiss me now?"

Gavin smiled, his large, strong hands embracing her face in warmth, and his mouth landed on hers, engulfing her in tender kisses. He teased and tempted, giving her glimpses of what was yet to come. Her heart surged with hope and happiness. Maybe this time it would be she who slayed the dragon, got the gold, and maybe even the knight in the process.

Placing his forehead on hers, he said softly against her lips, "You still taste like strawberries."

About the Author

Award-winning author Dominique Eastwick grew up a US Navy Brat, so if there was a naval base, that was probably home. She currently resides in North Carolina with her husband, two children, crazy lab and lazy cat.

Dominique's love of reading started when she was told to read *To Kill a Mockingbird* in high school. A book that opened her eyes to the joys of reading and entering into the world of the author. To this day she ranks this book as her favorite.

Stay connected with my Newsletter:
http://eepurl.com/brjq6D

Other Books by Dominique

The Duke and the Virgin

The Marquis and the Mistress

The Earl and His Virgin Countess

Infiltrating Her Pack

Shifting Hearts

Siren's Serenade

Healing His Soul's Mate

The Virgin's Infiltrator

Breaking the Mating Bond